MAGIC TREE HOUSE®

#31 WARRIORS IN WINTER

Dear Reader,

Did you know there's a Magic Tree House® book for every kid? From those just starting to read chapter books to more experienced readers, Magic Tree House® has something for everyone, including science, sports, geography, wildlife, history... and always a bit of mystery and magic!

Magic Tree House®
Adventures with Jack and Annie, perfect for readers who are just starting to read chapter books.
F&P Level: M

Magic Tree House®
Merlin Missions
More challenging adventures for the experienced Magic Tree House® reader.
F&P Levels: M–N

Magic Tree House®
Super Edition
A longer and more dangerous adventure with Jack and Annie.
F&P Level: P

Magic Tree House®
Fact Trackers
Nonfiction companions to your favorite Magic Tree House® adventures.
F&P Levels: N–X

Happy reading!

Mary Pope Osborne

MAGIC TREE HOUSE®

#31 WARRIORS IN WINTER

BY MARY POPE OSBORNE

ILLUSTRATED BY AG FORD

A STEPPING STONE BOOK™

Random House 🏠 New York

Text copyright © 2019 by Mary Pope Osborne
Jacket art and interior illustrations copyright © 2019 by AG Ford

All rights reserved. Published in the United States by Random House Children's Books, a division of Penguin Random House LLC, New York.

Random House and the colophon are registered trademarks and A Stepping Stone Book and the colophon are trademarks of Penguin Random House LLC.

Magic Tree House is a registered trademark of Mary Pope Osborne; used under license.

Visit us on the Web!
rhcbooks.com
MagicTreeHouse.com

Educators and librarians, for a variety of teaching tools, visit us at
RHTeachersLibrarians.com

Library of Congress Cataloging-in-Publication Data
Names: Osborne, Mary Pope, author. | Ford, AG, illustrator.
Title: Warriors in winter / by Mary Pope Osborne; illustrated by AG Ford.
Description: New York: Random House, [2019] | Series: Magic Tree House; #31 | "A Stepping Stone Book." | Summary: "The magic tree house whisks Jack and Annie back in time to meet famed Roman emperor Marcus Aurelius!" —Provided by publisher.
Identifiers: LCCN 2018025053 | ISBN 978-0-525-64764-5 (hardback) | ISBN 978-0-525-64765-2 (lib. bdg.) | ISBN 978-0-525-64766-9 (ebook)
Subjects: LCSH: Marcus Aurelius, Emperor of Rome, 121–180—Juvenile fiction. | CYAC: Marcus Aurelius, Emperor of Rome, 121–180—Fiction. | Kings, queens, rulers, etc.—Fiction. | Soldiers—Fiction. | Space and time—Fiction. | Magic—Fiction. | Tree houses—Fiction. | Rome—History—Empire, 30 B.C–284 A.D.—Fiction. | BISAC: JUVENILE FICTION / Action & Adventure / General. | JUVENILE FICTION / Fantasy & Magic. | JUVENILE FICTION / Historical / General.
Classification: LCC PZ7.O81167 War 2019 | DDC [Fic]—dc23

Printed in the United States of America
10 9 8 7 6 5 4 3 2 1

This book has been officially leveled by using the F&P Text Level Gradient™ Leveling System.

For Glenn "Chip" Hughes,
poet and philosopher

 CONTENTS

PROLOGUE

One summer day in Frog Creek, Pennsylvania, a mysterious tree house appeared in the woods. It was filled with books. A boy named Jack and his sister, Annie, found the tree house and soon discovered that it was magic. They could go to any time and place in history just by pointing to a picture in one of the books. While they were gone, no time at all passed back in Frog Creek.

Jack and Annie eventually found out that the tree house belonged to Morgan le Fay, a magical librarian from the legendary realm of Camelot.

Since then, they have traveled on many adventures in the magic tree house and completed many missions for Morgan.

On their journeys to New York and Texas, Jack and Annie learned great wisdom from two heroes of the recent past. Now they're about to journey *far* back in time to learn from a third hero!

1

WAY OF THE EAGLE

"Wake up, Jack."

Jack opened his eyes. The light was dim outside his window. His sister, Annie, was standing by his bed.

"What's going on?" he asked.

"I heard a weird sound outside," said Annie. "And guess what I saw!"

"What?" said Jack.

"An eagle!" said Annie. "A *huge* eagle. It was sitting on top of the lamppost in our yard."

"No way," said Jack.

"Yes, way," said Annie. "I'll bet Morgan sent him."

Jack sat up in bed. He threw off his covers. "I'm coming!" he said.

"Hurry. We have to get back home before Mom and Dad get up. Meet you on the porch." Annie slipped out of the room.

Jack climbed out of bed. He changed into his jeans, sweatshirt, and sneakers. He grabbed his backpack. Then he crept downstairs and went out to the front porch.

Annie was waiting in the chilly, damp air. Dawn was breaking.

"There!" she whispered. She pointed toward the lamppost in front of their house.

An eagle was perched on top. He was dark brown, except for a ring of golden-brown feathers around his neck. He stared at them with piercing eyes.

"Oh, man, that's a golden eagle," whispered Jack.

4

The eagle spread his wings. He rose into the early-morning sky and flew toward the woods.

"Follow him!" said Jack.

Jack and Annie ran down the porch steps. They crossed their yard and dashed down the sidewalk after the eagle.

"There!" said Annie, looking up. She pointed to the bird gliding above the Frog Creek woods.

Jack and Annie crossed the street. They hurried between the shadowy trees, until they came to the tallest oak.

"Whoa!" said Jack.

The eagle was perched on the roof of the magic tree house.

"Yay!" said Annie.

"You were right!" said Jack.

They climbed up the rope ladder and into the tree house.

Sunlight streamed onto the floor. It shined on two small wooden tablets. Next to the tablets was a scroll.

"A message from Morgan!" said Annie. She unrolled the scroll and read:

Land by the Danube
Many years ago.
Find a Roman legion camp
Dusted with snow.

"A *Roman legion camp*?" said Jack. "Really?"

"What's a legion?" said Annie.

"A legion is a unit in the ancient Roman army," said Jack. "A legion had almost six thousand warriors. The whole army had around 150,000 warriors. And—"

"Okay, got it," said Annie. "And what's the Danube?"

"It's a river that ran along the border of the Roman empire," said Jack. "That was almost two thousand years ago."

"How do you know all this?" said Annie.

"My school project on the Roman army," said Jack. "Remember that model of a camp I made? And I had to explain it to my class."

"Oh, yeah, I remember," said Annie.

"Rome had the best warriors in the world," said Jack. "They defended the Roman empire for over five hundred years! They—"

7

"Great, got it," said Annie. "There's more here from Morgan." She read from the scroll again:

You must each keep a journal.
Use tablets of wax.
With a pen called a stylus,
Write down the facts.

"So that's what *this* is!" said Jack. He grabbed one of the wooden tablets. "In ancient times, people wrote on these. See, the wood's covered with wax." He picked up a pointed reed. "And here's the stylus! It's like a pen with no ink!"

"Hold on," said Annie. "Listen to this."

Write what you see.
Write what you feel.
Do what warriors do
To make your words real.

8

"How do we 'do what warriors do'?" Jack said. "Roman warriors were the toughest guys on the planet. They had years of training."

"Maybe Morgan sent us something to give us magic skills," said Annie, "like the baseball caps we wore to be major league batboys."

They looked in the shadowy corners of the tree house. Jack saw only the Pennsylvania book that would bring them home.

"Nothing here," he said. "Morgan didn't even send a research book to help us."

"Don't worry, you know a lot from your project," said Annie.

"Not *enough*," said Jack.

"Well, maybe Morgan wants us to learn more on our own," said Annie. "Last verse."

Give the silver coin
To a hero in disguise.

He will share with you his wisdom.
Be home by moonrise.

"What silver coin?" said Annie.

They looked around the tree house again. Jack spotted a black coin on the floor. It was about the size of a quarter.

"Maybe this?" he said, picking it up.

"That doesn't look like silver," said Annie.

"Silver turns dark over time," said Jack. "You have to polish it."

"Okay, we can do that later. Let's go now!" said Annie.

"How?" said Jack. "There's no research book to take us to the right place."

"Hmm . . . ," said Annie. "I have an idea. I'll just point at Morgan's words." She touched the rhyme. "I wish we could go to a *Roman legion camp* on the *Danube*!"

10

A cry from the eagle pierced the air.
The wind started to blow.
The tree house started to spin.
It spun faster and faster.
Then everything was still.
Absolutely still.

2

RIDER ON A BLACK HORSE

The air was cold and bright.

"Brrr, it feels like winter," said Annie.

"Yeah," said Jack, shivering. He could see his breath in the frosty air. "We're wearing Roman clothes. Too bad they're not warmer."

Jack and Annie both wore wool capes with tunics and boots. Instead of a backpack, Jack had a leather pouch attached to a belt. Annie had a belt and pouch, too.

"Hey, I'm dressed like a boy," she said. "This should be fun."

They looked out the window. Snow covered the ground.

Sunlight sparkled on a frozen river.

"That must be the Danube," said Jack.

An eagle cried out. Annie leaned out the window and looked to the right. "Our eagle!" she said. "And that must be our Roman camp!"

Jack leaned out the window, too. He saw the eagle gliding toward a cluster of buildings surrounded by a high wooden fence.

"Oh, man, it looks like my model," said Jack.

"Yep, and it's *dusted with snow,* just like in Morgan's rhyme," said Annie. "Let's go!"

Jack and Annie put their tablets and pens in their leather pouches. Jack dropped the coin into his pouch, too. Then they climbed down the rope ladder.

The sunlight on the snow was blindingly bright. But the air was bitter cold. Jack pulled his cape closer. The thick wool was warm and scratchy.

"Before we go any farther, maybe we should write something in our journals," he said.

"Good idea," said Annie.

They pulled out their writing tools.

"Watch," said Jack. He pressed the pointed reed into the wax and wrote a *W*.

"Got it," said Annie. "But we should write small so we can fit everything in."

Jack wrote *WINTER*. Then he looked at Annie, writing her own notes.

"What are *you* writing?" he asked.

"Rider on a black horse," she said.

"Where?" Jack said, looking around.

"Against the sun," said Annie.

Jack shielded his eyes and looked at the bright horizon.

A rider on a black horse was trotting over the frozen ground between the river and the camp. He wore a helmet and a red cape.

Oh, no! thought Jack. *Should we climb back into the tree house?*

"Hi!" Annie called, waving.

The rider raised his hand in greeting. He

15

trotted over to them. His face was mostly hidden by his helmet.

"Hail, children! Are you lost?" he asked.

Jack was relieved. The man's voice was friendly.

"Not lost," said Annie. "Actually, we want to visit that army camp."

"Have you family there?" asked the warrior.

"No, we just want to learn more about the Roman legion," said Jack.

"We're keeping journals," said Annie. She held up her tablet and stylus.

"Indeed?" said the man. "You are the first children I have met who keep journals."

"We plan to write what we see and what we feel," said Annie.

"Ah, young visiting scholars," said the rider. "Have you questions for me?"

"Um . . . yes," said Jack. "Why is the army camped here?"

"Legion Gemina Fourteen is camped on the

Danube to protect Rome's northern border," said the rider. "To keep invaders from crossing the river."

"Who are the invaders?" asked Annie.

"Anyone who wants to take away our freedom," said the rider, "and destroy the Roman way of life."

"Do you know how we can get inside the camp?" said Jack.

"Give the guard the password of the day," the rider said. *"Mars the Victor."*

"Like Mars the planet?" asked Annie.

"No, like Mars, the Roman god of war," Jack said.

"Oh. Who's the Roman god of peace?" asked Annie.

"Pax is the goddess of peace," said the rider. His horse pawed the ground.

"Pax. I like that," said Annie.

"Tell the guard you plan to report on the legion's hard work," said the rider. "Say you are visiting scholars under the command of the Imperial Guard."

"'Visiting scholars under the command of the Imperial Guard,'" Jack repeated slowly. "Got it." *That sounds really official,* he thought.

The rider squinted at the rising sun. "I must return to my station now," he said. "Farewell, friends!"

The rider turned his horse and galloped toward the camp. Jack and Annie watched him pass through the gateway.

"Let's go!" said Jack, and they started walking toward the gate.

"He was nice," said Annie. "Do you think he was an important officer in the legion?"

"No way," said Jack. "He was just an ordinary army guy. He didn't have a plume on his helmet. And he didn't wear armor covered with medals, like a centurion. Be glad he *wasn't* a centurion."

"Why? What's a centurion?" asked Annie.

"Super-strict commanders," said Jack. "They carry big sticks to whack their own men."

"That's mean," said Annie. "They should learn to use their words instead."

Jack laughed. "Try telling that to a centurion."

As they drew close to the camp, a guard stepped out of the gatehouse. He wore full battle armor. He carried a spear and a red shield.

"Hail!" said Annie.

"Word of the day?" the guard said in a deep voice.

"Mars the Victor!" Annie answered.

Jack cleared his throat and called out, "We are visiting scholars under the command of the Imperial Guard!"

"We have come to write about the camp," said Annie. She held up her tablet and stylus. "We

plan to spread the word about the legion's hard work!"

The watchman lowered his spear. "Welcome to Legion Gemina Fourteen," he said, "in the reign of Emperor Marcus Aurelius!"

"Thank you!" said Annie.

She and Jack walked proudly past the guard. They passed through the gateway and entered the Roman camp.

3

WARRIORS AWAKE!

Annie and Jack stood on the main road. The road passed through the center of the camp. It was lined with rows of wooden buildings.

"Where is everybody?" Annie asked.

"I don't know," said Jack. "These buildings look like barracks. That's where warriors sleep."

"Oh. So maybe they're still asleep," said Annie.

"No chance," said Jack. "Roman warriors get up before dawn. Maybe they went on a march."

"Where did our guy on the black horse go?" said Annie.

"He disappeared," said Jack, looking around. "I wish we had a research book."

"Don't worry, you know a lot," said Annie.

"Not enough," said Jack.

"Let's explore and see what we can find out," said Annie.

Jack and Annie started down the stone road. They stopped at a flagpole.

A red flag was waving in the wind.

On the flag was the figure of a ram. Below the ram were two words: *Legion Gemina.* The words were followed by three capital letters: *XIV.*

"Those letters stand for the number fourteen," said Jack. "They're called Roman numerals."

"I actually knew that," said Annie. "Our teacher taught us Roman numerals."

"Cool," said Jack. Then they both made notes about the flag.

"Hey," said Annie. "Hear that noise?"

Jack listened. Sounds were coming from the far end of the camp. "Let's check it out," he said.

Jack and Annie hurried down the road. The sounds grew louder.

"Something's going on outside the walls," said Jack.

Jack and Annie hurried past the rows of barracks, until they came to the camp's rear gate. "Mars the Victor!" Annie called to a guard.

The guard waved them on, and they stepped through the gate onto a huge frosty field.

"Oh, man!" said Jack.

"Warriors! Finally!" said Annie.

Hundreds of men were training on the field. They all wore armor and helmets. They were running, boxing, wrestling, throwing spears, and shooting arrows at targets.

Not far away, a huge man was barking orders at a team of runners. He had a red plume on his

helmet and medals on his armor, and he waved a big stick.

"Hey—a centurion!" said Annie.

"Yep," Jack said.

"You gave a perfect description," said Annie.

"Double time!" the centurion yelled.

The runners ran twice as fast. They were wearing heavy armor with huge packs strapped to their backs.

"Remember how our rhyme says we should do what warriors do?" said Annie.

"Ha!" said Jack. "There's no way I can do what those guys are doing."

"Me neither," said Annie. "But let's get closer to them and take some notes." Their feet crunched over the frozen grass as they headed toward the runners.

"Halt!" a loud voice thundered. The tall, burly centurion had spotted them. He dropped his stick and pulled out his sword.

"Yikes," said Annie.

"Word of the day!" the huge man shouted, striding toward them. "Loud and clear!"

"Mars the Victor!" Jack shouted. His heart was pounding. "We're visiting scholars under the command of the Imperial Guard!"

"We're taking notes on the legion!" said Annie, holding up her tablet. "We want to report on your good work!"

The centurion studied them. Then he put away his sword. He pointed at the runners.

"Fighters in training!" he roared. "Best training in the world! Write it down!"

Jack's hand trembled as he took notes.

"What's in their packs?" Annie asked.

"Food, water, bedroll, pans, hand mill, spade, ax," the centurion shouted, "plus sixty pounds of weapons! Best weapons in the world! Write it down!"

Jack and Annie took notes.

"Do they train every day?" asked Jack.

"Of course!" said the centurion. "And three times a month, they march twenty miles with full armor and packs! If one gets out of step, he is punished. If he deserts his comrades, he is slain! Those are the rules."

Whoa, thought Jack.

"Are there any women soldiers?" asked Annie.

"Certainly not!" said the centurion. "Females have no fighting skills!"

"You don't know our aunt Sally," murmured Annie.

"Shush," said Jack.

"Well, she's a major in the army," said Annie. "And she has a black belt in karate."

The centurion didn't seem to hear her. "The cavalry trains there!" he yelled, pointing across the field.

Men on horseback were jumping over log fences. Jack looked for the rider on the black horse.

"Best horses in the world!" said the centurion. "Write it down!"

Jack and Annie wrote it down.

"What do warriors do when they're *not* training?" said Annie.

"Clean stables, dig ditches, cook meals," the man answered. "Repair armor, make weapons, build roads."

"I read that Romans make great roads," said Jack.

"Best in the world!" the man snapped. "Write it down!"

Jack and Annie wrote it down. Jack could see that Annie was trying not to laugh.

"We must prepare now for the royal parade," said the centurion. "The emperor arrived from Rome yesterday to review the legion. Good day!"

The centurion turned and strode back to his runners.

"Scary guy," said Annie.

"Typical centurion," said Jack, trying to sound calm. "Let's get out of here."

"Wait," said Annie. "What did you write?"

Jack read from his tablet:

WINTER, rows of barracks, red flag
    with ram,
best weapons, best horses, best roads

"Good," Annie said. "But the rhyme said: *Write what you feel.* You didn't do that."

"Well, what did you write?" said Jack.

"I wrote stuff like 'Rider on black horse friendly. Like him!' 'Love the red shields!'"

"Oh. Okay," said Jack. He pressed his stylus into his wax tablet. He wrote:

Nervous! Heart attack! Help!!!

Annie laughed when she read Jack's note.

"It's true! My heart's pounding!" he said.

"Let's go back inside," said Annie.

She and Jack left the field and hurried back into the legion camp.

4

No Skills

Jack and Annie stopped on the main road.

"Okay! We still have to try to do what warriors do," said Annie.

"And don't forget the part about the silver coin," said Jack.

"Give the silver coin to a hero in disguise," Annie quoted. *"He will share with you his wisdom. Be home by moonrise."*

"I wonder who the hero is," said Jack.

"What kind of Roman soldier wears a disguise?" asked Annie.

"I don't know," said Jack. "I told you I don't know enough."

"What's that?" Annie pointed to smoke rising from behind some of the barracks.

"Let's check it out," said Jack.

Jack and Annie walked down a path between two rows of barracks. The chilly air smelled of wood smoke and fish.

Soon they came to warriors working in a cooking area. Wearing simple tunics and capes, some of the men were grilling fish over campfires. Another was removing a loaf of bread from a stone oven. The oven looked like a giant beehive.

"Hey, we can do what he's doing," Annie said to Jack. "We know how to bake bread."

"Yeah," said Jack, "but we have an electric oven, and we use flour from the supermarket."

"Let's ask him how *they* do it," said Annie. "Hail!" she called to the bread baker.

The man looked up, startled.

"Mars the Victor!" Jack said. "We're visiting scholars—"

"Writing about the legion's good work," said Annie. "Are you the cook for the whole camp?"

35

The man laughed. "No, it is my week to do the baking for my squad," he said.

Jack leaned toward Annie. "Eight to ten guys in a squad," he said.

"What does your squad eat?" Annie asked the warrior.

He recited a list: "Cheese, beans, salted fish, olives, barley, bread."

"How do you make your bread?" Jack said.

"Each squad grinds its own portion of grain," said the baker. He pointed to a small hand mill next to the oven.

"Cool," said Annie. "Can we try?"

The man nodded. "There's a bit of grain in it now. Turn the handle to grind it. Flour will come out the spout."

Annie tried to turn the handle, but it wouldn't budge.

"You try," she said to Jack.

Jack pushed the handle as hard as he could.

He pushed and pushed. Finally a spoonful of flour came out of the spout.

"Your bread loaf will be the size of an olive," said the baker.

Jack and Annie laughed.

"You should ask Ceres for help, so you don't starve," the man said with a smile. He returned to his work.

"Who's Ceres?" Annie asked as they walked away.

"Goddess of grain," said Jack. "Ancient Romans had gods and goddesses for everything."

"Oh, like in Greek mythology?" said Annie.

"Right," said Jack. "Gods and goddesses for the sun, the sea, storms, sleep, rainbows . . ."

"Got it, got it," said Annie. "So Ceres is the Roman goddess of grain." She made a note.

"There's smoke coming from over there, too," said Jack. "Let's go."

They walked down the path to an open workshop.

At a forge, a blacksmith hammered a sword. Other men were making sandals, shields, and wagon wheels. The craftsmen were working so hard, they didn't seem to notice Jack and Annie.

"An eagle," whispered Annie. She pointed to a craftsman adding gold paint to a carved wooden eagle.

"That's the standard of a Roman legion," whispered Jack.

"What's a standard?" asked Annie.

"It's a symbol that stands for the legion," said Jack. "It's a great honor to carry the gold eagle. The person who does is called the standard-bearer."

"Cool," said Annie. "Hail!" she called to someone behind Jack.

Jack turned to look. The blacksmith was staring at them.

"Hail," the man said gruffly.

"Maybe *he'll* let us do what he's doing," Annie said softly. "We know how to hammer."

"Yeah, anyone can hammer," said Jack. He and Annie walked over to the blacksmith.

"We're visiting scholars," Annie said. "We're learning about the legion. May we try what you're doing?"

Without a word, the blacksmith handed her his hammer. It was so heavy, Annie fell to the ground with it.

The blacksmith laughed.

"Oops!" Annie said, getting to her feet. "Your turn," she said to Jack.

The hammer was lying on the ground. Jack tried to pick it up. He couldn't lift it higher than his knees. "No can do," he said. "We're wimps."

"We have no skills," said Annie.

The blacksmith nodded. He took back his hammer. "Pray to Vulcan," he said, and he went back to work on the sword.

"Who's Vulcan?" Annie asked Jack.

"The Roman god of fire and craftsmen," said Jack.

Annie made a note. "Maybe it's time to look for a hero in disguise," she said.

"Sure," said Jack. "But first, let's check out *that* building." He pointed to a long building near the back gate. "Maybe warriors are doing something in there that we could try."

"Okay," said Annie.

Jack and Annie put their writing tools into their pouches. Then they walked down the pathway to the open entrance of the building. They peeked inside.

"Oh, man!" whispered Jack. "The *armory*!"

5

GET IN LINE!

Winter sunlight shone on metal helmets and jackets. It shone on broad belts, swords, daggers, spears, and red-and-gold-painted shields.

"No one's in here," said Annie.

"That's weird," said Jack.

"Or lucky," said Annie. She grinned at him. "Finally we can do what warriors do."

"What? You mean we should try on their armor?" said Jack.

Annie nodded.

"Everything will be too big," said Jack.

"Who cares?" said Annie. "No one will see us."

"Right," Jack said nervously. He really wanted to try on the armor. "Actually, it might not be *too* big. A Roman soldier had to be at least five feet six inches. That's only five inches taller than me. And about eight inches taller than you. So if we—"

"Got it! Let's do it!" said Annie.

"Okay!" said Jack. "Quick, before anyone shows up."

Jack and Annie hurried through the wide entrance of the armory. They pulled off their capes and dropped them on the ground.

"Where do we start?" said Annie.

They looked around at shelves lined with body armor and helmets. In the center of the room were weapons and shields on wooden stands.

"Upper body armor," said Jack. He crossed to a shelf with metal jackets. The jackets were made of overlapping strips of iron. "This one looks pretty small."

He lifted the gray metal jacket off the shelf. "Whoa! It's heavy!"

Annie held out her arms. Jack helped her slide the armor over her tunic. The jacket reached her knees!

"Help!" she said, nearly sinking to the floor.

Jack laughed. "You look like a cartoon character," he said.

"It's *crazy* heavy!" said Annie.

"Want to take it off?" said Jack.

"Not yet," she said. "Put yours on."

Jack chose one of the metal jackets for himself and slipped his arms into it. The metal was freezing cold!

"Oh, man, how can warriors run or fight in this?" said Jack. "It weighs a ton!"

"And they march with really heavy packs on their backs, too!" said Annie.

"And carry shields!" said Jack. "Huge shields!"

"Unbelievable!" said Annie.

44

"Now helmets!" said Jack. He studied the row of helmets.

He picked one for himself and lowered it onto his head. "Oh, man, at least another fifteen pounds!" he said.

"Let me try one," said Annie.

Jack picked a helmet for Annie and lowered it onto her head.

"Help!" she squeaked. "I can hardly see or hear." Annie's helmet partially covered her eyes, ears, cheeks, and mouth.

Jack laughed. "I can hardly see, either," he said. "But I feel braver wearing this stuff. Don't you?"

"No," said Annie. "I'm dying in here." Her voice was muffled.

"Okay, let's take everything off," said Jack.

Suddenly voices and the sound of running feet came from outside.

"Full armor! No packs!" a man shouted. "Emperor's parade begins at high noon!"

"Yikes," said Annie.

"Get out of their way!" Jack said in a panic. He pulled Annie into the shadows.

Warriors poured into the armory. Jack recognized the cooks and craftsmen among the others.

"Mars the Victor," Annie said. Her voice was muffled inside her helmet.

"Quiet!" Jack whispered.

"Belts! Helmets! Shields!" someone bellowed. A stocky centurion stood at the entrance of the armory.

Oh, no, thought Jack. *Another centurion!*

"Double time!" the man roared.

The warriors moved quickly down the shelves, gathering metal jackets, helmets, and military belts.

"Everyone in line! *Now!*" the centurion shouted.

The warriors grabbed weapons and shields. The armory was filled with loud voices and clanking metal.

47

"We have to get out of here!" Jack said to Annie. "We can take everything off outside! Let's go!"

"I can't see!" Annie said.

"I'll lead you!" Jack said.

Jack took Annie's hand. Stumbling awkwardly in their heavy armor, they moved with the warriors toward the entrance.

"Line up!" the centurion bellowed. "Single file!"

The warriors almost knocked Jack and Annie over as they all spilled out into the bright sunlight.

6

DESERTERS!

Jack pulled Annie to the side of the armory. "We'll stay here till they're gone," he said.

Annie nodded.

The warriors were joining a parade line. The line stretched all the way to the main road.

"Prepare to march!" the centurion shouted.

A horn sounded, and the warriors started jogging down the path.

"Come on, let's get out of this stuff," Jack said to Annie. "Before we get caught!"

Jack yanked off his helmet. He unlaced his metal jacket and pulled it off.

"Whew!" he said. He felt light enough to float through the air!

"Help!" said Annie. Her helmet was off, but she was struggling to get out of her metal jacket.

"Hold on," said Jack.

Jack helped Annie unlace the jacket and take it off.

"There! Great!" said Annie. "Now we'd better—"

"Deserters!" someone shouted.

Jack and Annie whirled around. In the distance, a centurion was pointing at them.

"Oh, no! He must think we're soldiers trying to escape from the legion!" said Jack.

"Deserters!" the centurion shouted again. "Get them!"

"Time to go!" said Jack.

"Run!" said Annie.

She and Jack ran in the opposite direction of the centurion and the parade line. They zigzagged between barracks until they came to the main road.

At the far end of the road, warriors were lining up at the back gate.

"The front gate!" called Jack.

They charged up the main road, heading for the entrance of the camp.

"Halt!"

Jack looked back. Several horsemen were riding toward them.

"Halt!" the lead horseman shouted again.

"Keep going!" Jack shouted to Annie. "Double time!"

Jack and Annie ran as fast as they could.

An arrow whizzed past them.

"Stop!" Jack shouted to Annie. "*Stop!*"

Annie stopped.

"We have to explain!" Jack said breathlessly. "Turn around! Put your hands up!"

Holding up their hands, Jack and Annie turned to face the horsemen.

The leader was a centurion. He wore a crested helmet and a red cape.

"Mars the Victor!" Jack yelled. "We're visiting

scholars! Under the Imperial Guard! We come in peace!"

"Pax!" Annie shouted. "Pax!"

The warriors on horseback circled them. Jack felt very small.

The centurion leaned forward. "What tribe are you from?" he barked.

"Uh . . . Frog Creek!" Jack blurted out.

"Frog Creek?" the centurion said. "There is no such tribe."

"Perhaps they came across the river from the north," said another warrior. "They are very small."

"Did you cross the Danube?" the centurion asked.

"Uh . . . actually, I don't know where Frog Creek is exactly in relation to your camp," said Jack. "But it's possibly . . . um . . ."

"Who told you the secret word of the day?" the centurion demanded.

"A rider on a black horse," said Annie.

"Where did you see him?" the man asked.

"Outside the camp," said Annie. "He was alone."

"Our warriors do not ride alone outside the camp! What did he tell you?" asked the centurion.

"He told us to make notes about the Roman legion. And that's what we've been doing all day—taking notes," said Jack.

"So a rider on a black horse gave you our secret daily password?" the centurion said.

"Yes, sir," said Jack.

"And he told you to write about our camp?" said the centurion.

"Yes," said Jack.

"And you don't know his name," the centurion said.

"He didn't tell us his name. But he must be here somewhere," said Annie. "He rode into the camp."

"He is *here*? He rode into our camp?" The centurion turned to the other horsemen. "An enemy spy is inside our walls!" he roared.

"No, not an *enemy*!" said Annie. "Not a *spy*!"

The horsemen ignored her and all began yelling at once:

"He is here!"

"Rode into our camp!"

"An enemy spy!"

"Inside our walls!"

"We must stop the parade!" the centurion roared. The horsemen stared at their leader. "Zeno, alert Emperor Aurelius!"

One of the horsemen nodded and galloped off.

"We will take these prisoners to the royal tent," said the centurion. "The emperor will decide their fate!"

7

LORD EMPEROR AURELIUS

"March!" the centurion ordered. He pointed toward the back gate.

With the centurion leading them and horsemen on either side, Jack and Annie started down the road.

The midday sun still shone brightly, but the wind had picked up. Jack shivered from the cold—and from fear. He'd read about Roman emperors. Some were ruthless and cruel. Some were truly insane. All of them got rid of their enemies, one way or another.

"I wish we could find our guy on the black horse," Jack said in a low voice to Annie. "Before *they* find him."

"I'm sure he wasn't a spy," said Annie.

"Me too," said Jack. "But who was he? And where did he go?"

"Quiet!" yelled a horseman.

The centurion led them through the back gate. They stepped out onto the training field.

"Oh, man," whispered Jack.

On the field, the whole legion stood in parade formation. Six thousand armored warriors were lined up in perfect rows. The warriors were as still as statues. Each held a red-and-gold shield with his left hand and a spear with his right.

Trumpeters stood near the head of the parade. In front of them was a warrior carrying the legion's red flag. In front of him was a man carrying a pole with a statue of a gold eagle on top.

"To the imperial tent!" the centurion ordered Jack and Annie. He pointed to a large red tent on the far side of the field. A cluster of guards stood around the entrance.

"Double time!" the centurion said.

As Jack and Annie hurried toward the tent, Jack grew even more scared.

Annie seemed scared, too. "Have you read much about Roman emperors?" she asked Jack.

"A little," said Jack.

"What did you learn?" said Annie.

"They're . . . okay," said Jack. "Don't worry."

"I'm not worried," said Annie. "I know we'll be fine!"

"Right!" said Jack. *Annie never gives up hope,* he thought. He liked that.

When they reached the entrance of the tent, the centurion dismounted.

"We have come to see the emperor!" he said to the guards. "We have captured two spies."

"Yes. Your messenger told us," said a guard. "He is with the emperor now. You may enter."

The guard pulled back the flap of the red tent. The centurion led Jack and Annie inside.

It was warm inside the tent. A fire was burning in a small iron stove. Tall candles cast shadows on silk curtains and woven carpets. Statues and maps were everywhere.

The messenger Zeno stood at attention.

Near him, a man sat on a heavy wooden chair set on a platform. He wore a long purple cloak with a gold clasp at the shoulder. His light brown hair and beard were curly.

The centurion bowed before the man.

"My Lord Emperor Aurelius," he said.

"Hail, Junius," said the emperor.

"Our camp has been invaded by spies, my lord," said the centurion. "I have captured these two, and I believe there is a third hiding among us."

"Yes. The messenger you sent has warned me,"

the emperor said. He narrowed his eyes and looked at Jack and Annie. His piercing gaze reminded Jack of something. . . . Was it the golden eagle on the lamppost at dawn?

"I'm—I'm sorry, my Lord Aurelius," stammered Jack. "We'd like to explain—"

Before Jack could go on, Annie burst out laughing. "Oh, wow!" she said.

"What?" said Jack.

"I can't believe it!" said Annie. She gave the emperor a big grin. "Hail, friend!"

Has Annie lost her mind? Jack wondered. "Stop! What's wrong with you?" he whispered.

"Don't you get it?" she said.

"Get what?" said Jack.

"It's *him*!" said Annie. "He's our guy! The rider on the black horse! He's not a spy! He's the emperor!"

Jack stared at the emperor. He couldn't

remember what the rider had looked like. Most of his face had been covered by his helmet.

"Junius, you and Zeno may leave us now. There is no danger of spies in our camp," the emperor said.

The centurion and the messenger looked confused, but they bowed and left the tent.

The emperor looked at Jack and Annie. "Hail, fellow scholars," he said. "Are you lost?"

8

THE SILVER COIN

Jack caught his breath. Emperor Aurelius *was* their guy! He couldn't believe it!

"No, not lost," said Annie, smiling. "We were just in the wrong place at the wrong time."

"The armory," explained Jack.

"So I hear," said the emperor. "When I first met you, I thought you must live nearby in Carnuntum. But now I do not think that is so. Where is your home?"

"Frog Creek, Pennsylvania," said Annie.

"Beyond the Danube," said Jack.

"Where are your horses?" the emperor asked.

"We left them . . . uh . . . on the other side of the river," said Jack.

"Yes, we walked across the ice," said Annie.

"But we're definitely not invaders or spies," said Jack quickly. "I promise. We wanted to learn about the Roman legion just for our own sake."

"I believe you," said the emperor. "When I spoke with you on my ride, I knew you were honest and trustworthy."

"Do you ride alone every morning?" asked Annie.

"When I can," said the emperor. "I like to look closely at the world around me and think my own thoughts."

"We like to look at the world, too," said Annie, "and write down our thoughts."

"And facts," added Jack.

"We tried to do that today when we wrote in our journals," said Annie.

"Ah, yes, and what did you write?" asked the emperor.

"I wrote about the weather," said Annie. "I made notes about the Roman gods. I even wrote a poem about two of them."

"Really? I should very much like to hear it," said the emperor.

"Sure," said Annie. She quoted from memory:

The weapons of Mars are heavy to bear.
But the peace of Pax is lighter than air.

The emperor nodded. "Lovely," he said. He looked at Jack.

"I wrote about the flag and the warriors' training," said Jack. "And I wrote about making bread and swords."

"Tell him what you wrote about having a heart attack," Annie said, smiling.

"Oh. I was a little nervous," said Jack. "And I wanted to make my sister laugh."

The emperor nodded. "So you both write honestly with poetry and humor, and you study the world closely."

"We try," said Annie.

"Those are useful and honorable qualities," said the emperor. "You are simple, brave, and honest. With training, you could be excellent warriors."

"Not me," said Annie. "I don't like to fight."

"Sometimes one must fight for the right things," said the emperor.

"Like what?" said Jack.

"Freedom and justice," said the emperor. "Truth."

"Are you ever scared?" asked Jack.

"Oh, yes," said the emperor. "But if I look deep within myself, I often find a hidden source of strength."

"That makes sense," said Annie.

"If I pretend to be a very brave person, I suddenly find that I am one," said the emperor.

"That makes sense, too," said Jack. "I felt brave for a moment when I put on warrior armor."

"In life we wear many disguises," said the emperor. "I sometimes feel I wear the disguise of a powerful emperor."

Annie gasped. *"Disguise!"* she whispered to Jack. "Hero in disguise! Silver coin!"

"Oh, man! Yes!" breathed Jack. He took out the black coin. "We want to give this to you," he said, handing the coin to the emperor.

"We think it's made of silver," said Annie.

The emperor looked at the coin. He crossed to a table with jars and poured some liquid onto a cloth. Then he rubbed the coin, polishing it. Soon the silver shone brightly.

The emperor held the coin close to a lantern

and studied it. He turned to Jack and Annie with a look of amazement. "Where did you get this?" he asked.

"Uh ... we ... found it in some woods," said Annie.

"Why? Is there something wrong with it?" said Jack.

"This coin is in honor of *me*," said the emperor. "Its engraving shows me with my warriors on a frozen river. It looks as if we have had a great victory on the Danube."

"You don't remember?" said Jack, confused.

"I do not," said the emperor in a hushed voice. "Because this battle has not yet happened. Look at the date." He handed the coin to Jack.

Jack and Annie studied the Roman numerals.

"It says 173," said Jack.

"Indeed it does," said the emperor. "But we are now in the year of 172."

"Oh," said Annie. "Well, that doesn't make sense."

"No. Unless . . ." The emperor looked at Jack and Annie with his golden eagle gaze. "It is a coin from the *future*."

9

MARCH!

"From the *future*?" said Jack. He and Annie looked at each other.

"How could that be? That's amazing," Annie said to the emperor.

"Unbelievable," said Jack.

"I do not understand," said the emperor. "Is this a sign from the gods? A gift from Mars? Perhaps it means that the legion should confront the enemy on the frozen Danube—take them by surprise—and stop their invasion."

"Sounds like a good plan to me," said Jack.

"It does," said Annie.

The emperor looked at them with wonder. "I do not know what to say to you," he said. "I would like to talk further. About your country. Your tribe. Perhaps you can stay awhile with the legion. I feel you may have much to teach me."

"I'm afraid we can't. We have a family back home," said Annie.

"We really need to be home by moonrise," said Jack.

"Ah," said the emperor. "I understand. But I am sorry to hear that. The moon rises early in winter."

The centurion Junius entered the tent. "My Lord Aurelius, the warriors are waiting. Shall I cancel the parade?"

"Of course not," said the emperor. "My honored guests, Jack and Annie, will march with you."

We will? Oh, no! thought Jack.

"Wait here," the emperor said to Jack and Annie. He stepped outside to talk with Junius.

"I hope he doesn't want us to carry shields and weapons," Jack said to Annie.

"Or wear armor," said Annie.

"No way!" said Jack. "We need an excuse!"

The emperor returned. "Go with Junius," he said to Jack and Annie. "He will show you what to do."

"Oh—" said Jack. Before he could think of an excuse, Junius beckoned for him and Annie to follow. The centurion led them out of the tent. They silently walked with him back to the parade line.

Jack's heart raced. *We can't march*, he thought. *We're too small! We're not strong enough!*

At the field, the legion was still standing in formation, waiting for the order to march. Junius walked over to the standard-bearer and flag-bearer. He turned to Jack and Annie.

"The emperor has ordered that the two of you shall carry the eagle standard and the flag. Which one of you wishes to carry the standard?" he said.

Oh, man, thought Jack. He knew this was the highest honor a Roman warrior could have. "You should carry it," he said to Annie.

"No, *you*," she said.

"You deserve it more," said Jack. He looked at the centurion. "Annie's very brave, and she never loses hope."

The standard-bearer handed the eagle standard to Annie.

"Wow, thanks," said Annie.

She held the pole high and smiled. The gold eagle's wings shone in the cold sunlight.

The flag-bearer handed Jack the flagpole. Jack raised it beside the eagle standard. The red flag with the ram flapped in the winter wind.

Trumpets sounded.

"You are to lead the legion once around the field," Junius said to Jack and Annie. "All the soldiers will follow you. March!"

Jack and Annie marched around the field with all of Legion Gemina XIV following them.

Annie carried the eagle standard.

Jack carried the red flag with the ram.

They were followed by trumpet players

who were followed by centurions

who were followed by thousands

and thousands of Roman warriors.

Jack and Annie returned to the emperor. They gave the standard and the flag to Junius.

"Well done," said Emperor Aurelius. "I know you must leave us now. I will ride with you as far as the riverbank."

The emperor gestured to a warrior standing beside a beautiful white horse. The horse had a red blanket draped over its back.

The warrior led the horse to Jack and Annie and helped them climb on. Jack took the reins.

Emperor Aurelius mounted his black horse.

As both horses started toward the gate, Jack gripped the reins and Annie held on to Jack. The white horse carried them down the main road past the armory, past the rows of barracks, and out through the front gate of the Roman legion camp.

10

HAIL, HOME!

Not far from the Danube River, the emperor dismounted. He helped Jack and Annie down from the white horse.

"Thank you for letting me carry the eagle, my Lord Aurelius," said Annie.

"You need not call me that outside the camp," said the emperor. "You may call me Marcus."

"Thanks for helping us, Marcus," said Jack.

"You're welcome," said Marcus. "I hope you learned about the Roman Legion today."

"We did," said Jack.

"You guys are amazing," said Annie. "We wrote a lot in our journals."

The emperor smiled. "Good," he said. "I tell few people this, but I myself keep a journal."

"Really?" Annie said. "What sort of things do you write?"

Marcus paused for a moment. "Perhaps I will share some of my thoughts with you," he said. He pulled his journal from a saddlebag. He read:

Dwell on the beauty of life.
Watch the stars, and see yourself
running with them.

"It sounds like poetry," said Jack.

"I love it," said Annie.

"Then perhaps you will like this, too," said Marcus. "I have begun a list of small things that have a special beauty for me." He read from his journal again:

MARY POPE OSBORNE

fresh bread
ripe figs
wheat bending in the field
the face of a lion
the beauty of old age in men
    and women
the smell of wood smoke

Marcus looked at them almost shyly.

"That's an amazing list, Marcus," said Jack.

"A beautiful list," said Annie.

"Thank you," said Marcus. He sighed. "I must

leave you now and don my emperor disguise again. There are battles still to be won."

"Good luck, Marcus," said Jack.

The emperor mounted his black horse. Jack handed him the reins of the white horse.

"Farewell, my friends," said Marcus. "I bid you safe travels."

"Thank you," said Jack.

"You should keep writing, Marcus," said Annie. "Your journal is really good."

The emperor smiled again and raised his hand. Then he turned and led the white horse back toward the camp.

"Let's go," Jack said to Annie. They hurried to the tree with the hidden tree house.

"Look," Annie said. She pointed up.

Jack saw the golden eagle perched high on a branch. "Hi, there," he said. Then he and Annie climbed up the rope ladder. They looked out the window together.

They watched the emperor pass through the front gate into the camp. The eagle cried out from above and flew into the darkening winter sky.

"It's time for Marcus to be ruler of the Roman Empire again," said Annie.

"Yup," said Jack. He took his tablet out of his pack and put it on the floor of the tree house. "Time for us to be Frog Creek kids again."

"Right," said Annie. She set her tablet beside Jack's. "We'll leave these for Morgan."

Jack picked up the Pennsylvania book. He pointed to a photo of the Frog Creek woods.

"I wish we could go there!" he said.

The wind started to blow.

The tree house started to spin.

It spun faster and faster.

Then everything was still.

Absolutely still.

❄ ❄ ❄

"Hail, home!" said Jack.

"Pax," Annie said with a sigh.

They were wearing their own clothes again. The sun was rising over the woods. Birds were singing.

"I hope Morgan likes our notes," said Jack, glancing at the tablets on the floor.

"I think she will," said Annie. "We should head home now and hop back into bed."

"Yep," said Jack. "Pretend to wake up when Mom calls us for breakfast."

"I hope Dad makes blueberry pancakes," said Annie.

"Best in the world!" said Jack.

"Write it down!" said Annie.

They laughed, then climbed down the rope ladder and started through the woods.

Jack felt a chilly morning breeze. "I'm glad we don't have to be Roman warriors," he said.

"Me too," said Annie. "But you know what's weird?"

"What?" said Jack. "Besides traveling through time and space in a magic tree house and spending the day in a Roman Legion camp?"

Annie laughed. "No, seriously," she said. "It's weird that the most important Roman warrior of that time made a list of small things of beauty."

"Yeah," said Jack. "Not what you'd expect."

"I think that might be the wisdom we were supposed to learn," said Annie.

"Right," said Jack.

"So what would you add to the list?" said Annie.

"Oh . . . maybe like . . ." Jack looked around. "Sunrays slanting between the trees."

"Fiddlehead ferns," said Annie.

"Leaves dancing in the breeze," said Jack.

"That dove cooing," said Annie.

"The eyes of an eagle," said Jack.

They came out of the woods and headed down the sidewalk.

"That black cat hiding in the bushes," said Annie.

"The Johnsons' pug on their porch," said Jack.

"Hi, Pickles!" Annie said in a loud whisper.

"Dandelions growing in a crack in the sidewalk," said Jack.

When they came to their house, they climbed the steps, crept inside, and tiptoed upstairs.

"See ya," they whispered to each other, and slipped into their rooms.

Jack changed back into his pajamas. Before he got into bed, he grabbed one of his books about ancient Rome. He looked in the index and found *Marcus Aurelius*.

He found the right page and read:

Marcus Aurelius was a Roman emperor from 161 to 180. He was a skillful military leader, but he is best known as a deep thinker who sought truth and wisdom. He recorded his private

thoughts in a journal called *Meditations.* The journal of Marcus Aurelius is still read more than 1,800 years after his death.

Below the passage was a quote from Marcus Aurelius:

"When you arise in the morning, think of what a precious privilege it is to be alive, to think, to enjoy, to love. . . ."

"No problem," whispered Jack. He smiled as he put the book back on the shelf. He climbed into bed, closed his eyes, and waited for his mom to call him to breakfast.

Pax.

Turn the page for a sneak peek at

Magic Tree House® Fact Tracker

Warriors

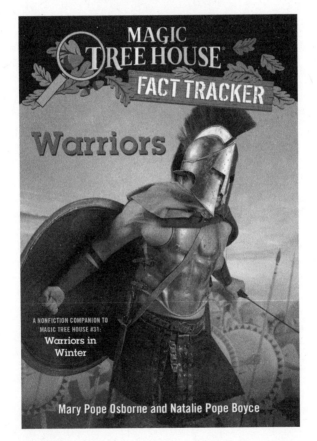

Ramses II, His Blue Crown, and the Lion

Ramses II is called Ramses the Great because he was a powerful warrior who won many battles for Egypt. He was also a great pharaoh who made the country stronger.

There are paintings of Ramses II wearing a double crown of red and white. The crowns were a symbol that he ruled all of Egypt.

Ramses II led his men into battle wearing a blue crown. There were stories that he also brought his pet

lioness along for luck! (Maybe it was an
ocelot. . . . What do you think?)

Ancient Greek Warriors

Ancient Greece had over a thousand city-states. The city-state of Athens was one of the most powerful.

Around 500 BCE, Athens created the first democracy. In a democracy, people can vote. The United States borrowed some ideas for its democracy from Greece.

Athenians produced wonderful art, buildings, poetry, plays, and stories.

The Greeks held the first Olympic games almost 3,000 years ago.

Alexander Spreads Greek Culture

Alexander, the son of King Philip of Macedonia, was one of the greatest warriors ever. He lived over 2,000 years ago. Philip ruled all of Greece. The famous Greek philosopher Aristotle was one of Alexander's teachers.

Alexander was twenty when he became king in 336 BCE. He set out to conquer more land. For thirteen years, he and his army of about 50,000 soldiers took over lands that stretched from Greece to India.

Alexander brought Greek ideas, arts, and customs to all the lands he conquered.

Alexander never lost a single battle, and he became known as Alexander the Great. He named seventy cities after himself and one after his horse Bucephalus (byoo-SEFF-uh-liss)! Alexander died of a fever when he was only thirty-three.

Caesar and the Pirates

When Julius Caesar was a young man, pirates captured a boat he was on. They asked his family for money to set him free. Caesar laughed at the small amount they wanted. He thought he was worth a lot more. He demanded that the pirates ask for more . . . and they did!

Caesar bossed the pirates around and made them listen to him practicing speeches and reciting poetry. He joined their games and exercised with them. At night, he told them to stop talking so he could sleep!

When Caesar was freed, he quickly commanded a boat, sailed back, and arrested all the pirates and had them put to death.

Chandragupta
340–297 BCE

Chandragupta lived in northern India over 2,000 years ago. Not much is known about his childhood, but stories say he was raised by peacock tamers!

When he was young, Chandragupta studied with a famous teacher named Chanakya, who taught him many things, including military strategy. After Alexander's army left India, Chandragupta raised an army and conquered Punjab.

With his large army and as many as 9,000 war elephants, Chandragupta won many more victories. His empire was known as the Mauryan Empire. It covered what is now Pakistan, Afghanistan, and most of India.

When he was an old man, Chandragupta gave up his throne and all of his riches to live as a poor monk.

Magic Tree House®

Magic Tree House®
Merlin Missions

Magic Tree House®
Super Editions

#1: WORLD AT WAR, 1944

Magic Tree House®
Fact Trackers

DINOSAURS

KNIGHTS AND CASTLES

MUMMIES AND PYRAMIDS

PIRATES

RAIN FORESTS

SPACE

TITANIC

TWISTERS AND OTHER TERRIBLE STORMS

DOLPHINS AND SHARKS

ANCIENT GREECE AND THE OLYMPICS

AMERICAN REVOLUTION

SABERTOOTHS AND THE ICE AGE

PILGRIMS

ANCIENT ROME AND POMPEII

TSUNAMIS AND OTHER NATURAL DISASTERS

POLAR BEARS AND THE ARCTIC

SEA MONSTERS

PENGUINS AND ANTARCTICA

LEONARDO DA VINCI

GHOSTS

LEPRECHAUNS AND IRISH FOLKLORE

RAGS AND RICHES: KIDS IN THE TIME OF
   CHARLES DICKENS

SNAKES AND OTHER REPTILES

DOG HEROES

ABRAHAM LINCOLN

PANDAS AND OTHER ENDANGERED SPECIES

HORSE HEROES

HEROES FOR ALL TIMES

SOCCER

NINJAS AND SAMURAI

CHINA: LAND OF THE EMPEROR'S GREAT
   WALL

SHARKS AND OTHER PREDATORS

VIKINGS

DOGSLEDDING AND EXTREME SPORTS

DRAGONS AND MYTHICAL CREATURES

WORLD WAR II

BASEBALL

WILD WEST

TEXAS

WARRIORS

More Magic Tree House®

GAMES AND PUZZLES FROM THE TREE HOUSE

MAGIC TRICKS FROM THE TREE HOUSE

MY MAGIC TREE HOUSE JOURNAL

MAGIC TREE HOUSE SURVIVAL GUIDE

ANIMALS GAMES AND PUZZLES

MAGIC TREE HOUSE INCREDIBLE FACT BOOK